Desert Animals

by Alison Auch

Content and Reading Adviser: Mary Beth Fletcher, Ed.D.
Educational Consultant/Reading Specialist
The Carroll School, Lincoln, Massachusetts

Spyglass
BOOKS

COMPASS POINT BOOKS

Minneapolis, Minnesota

Compass Point Books
3109 West 50th Street, #115
Minneapolis, MN 55410

Visit Compass Point Books on the Internet at *www.compasspointbooks.com*
or e-mail your request to *custserv@compasspointbooks.com*

Photographs ©: John Gerlach/Tom Stack and Associates, cover; Dave Watts/Tom Stack & Associates, 4;
Mark Newman/Visuals Unlimited, 5; Photo Network/Mark Newman, 6; Tom Stack/Tom Stack &
Associates, 7; Charles Melton/Visuals Unlimited, 8; DigitalVision, 9; J. Nutkowitz/Optiques
Photographic, 10; James P. Rowan, 11; Mary Ann McDonald, 12; Joe McDonald, 13, 17, 20 (bottom),
21 (top); Rod Williams/Bruce Coleman Inc., 14; Ken Lucas/Visuals Unlimited, 15; James E. Gerholdt,
16, 18; Joe McDonald/Tom Stack & Associates, 19; Photowood Inc./Corbis, 20 (top); William Dow/
Corbis, 20 (middle); Bill Leaman/The Image Finders, 21 (bottom).

Project Manager: Rebecca Weber McEwen
Editors: Heidi Schoof and Patricia Stockland
Photo Researcher: Svetlana Zhurkina
Designer: Jaime Martens

Library of Congress Cataloging-in-Publication Data
Auch, Alison.
  Desert animals / by Alison Auch.
    p. cm. — (Spyglass books)
Summary: Introduces some of the animals that live in a desert and how
they survive in such a harsh habitat.
Includes bibliographical references (p.   ).
  ISBN 0-7565-0445-7 (hardcover)
  1. Desert animals—Juvenile literature. [1. Desert animals.] I.
Title. II. Series.
  QL116 .A83 2003
  591.754—dc21   2002012621

Contents

NOTE: Glossary words are in **bold** the first time they appear.

Welcome to the Desert

Deserts are dry places.

Animals that live in
the desert do not need
much water.

Did You Know?

Most desert animals hunt for food at night when it is cool.

Foxy Friends

Foxes can live in the desert.

They get water from
the lizards and bugs they eat.

Did You Know?

Fennec foxes live in *burrows* during the day to stay cool.

That Stings

Scorpions can live in the desert.

They hunt **insects** and spiders at night.

Did You Know?

Scorpions use the stingers on their tails to kill their *prey.*

9

Fish in the Desert?

Pupfish can live in the desert.

They can live in very
hot water.

Did You Know?

Some deserts have streams, pools, and springs. Pupfish live in these places.

Jumping Rats

Kangaroo rats can live in the desert.

They get water from the seeds they eat.

Did You Know?

A kangaroo rat has long, strong back legs. It jumps like a real kangaroo.

Meow

Sand cats can live in the desert.

They use their large ears to hear small animals that they hunt for food.

Did You Know?

Sand cats have thick fur on their feet to keep out the hot sand.

It's a Monster!

Gila monsters can live in the desert.

They store fat in their tails. They live off this fat if they cannot find food.

Did You Know?

Gila monsters kill small animals with their *poisonous* bite.

Shake Shake Shake

Rattlesnakes can live in the desert.

They eat small animals. They sleep in their dens between their meals.

Did You Know?

Rattlesnakes use their rattles to scare off *enemies.* Rattlesnake bites are poisonous!

19

Fun Facts

The biggest desert in the world is the Sahara desert. It is in *Africa.*

Scorpions glow when a special light is shined on them.

Gila monsters are one of only two kinds of poisonous lizards in the whole world.

Kangaroo rats have *pouches* on the outside of their cheeks. They use the pouches to carry food back to their burrows.

Road runners can run as fast as 20 miles (32 kilometers) per hour.

Glossary

Africa–one of the seven continents

burrows–tunnels or holes made or used by an animal

enemies–those who want to hurt or kill others

insects–small, six-legged animals

poisonous–something that can kill or harm if it is eaten or touched

pouches–flaps of skin that can be used like bags or pockets

prey–animals that are hunted by other animals for food

Learn More

Books

Baker, Alan. *The Desert (Look Who Lives In).* New York: Peter Bedrick Books, 1999.

Gibson, Barbara. *Creatures of the Desert World.* Washington, D.C.: National Geographic Society, 1995.

Greenaway, Frank. *Look Closer: Desert Life.* New York: DK Publishing, 1992.

Web Sites

Brain POP

www.brainpop.com/science/seeall.weml (click on "desert")

Animal Planet—Rattlesnake Quiz

http://animal.discovery.com/ convergence/snakes/quiz/quiz.html

Index

GR: F

Word Count: 134

From Alison Auch

Reading and writing are my favorite things to do. When I'm not reading or writing, I like to go to the mountains or play with my little girl, Chloe.